For my sister, a friend of pill bugs —E.K.

This book is for Heina. —C.G.

 Published in the United States by Schwartz & Wade Books, an imprint of Random House Children's Books, a division of Penguin Random House LLC, New York. ★ Schwartz & Wade Books and the colophon are trademarks of Penguin Random House LLC. ★ Visit us on the Web! randomhousekids.com ★ Educators and librarians, for a variety of teaching tools, visit us at RHTeachersLibrarians.com

Library of Congress Cataloging-in-Publication Data Names: Kuhlman, Evan, author. | Groenink, Chuck, illustrator. Title: Hank's big day : the story of a bug / by Evan Kuhlman ; illustrated by Chuck Groenink. Description: First Edition. | New York : Schwartz & Wade Books, [2016] | Summary: Hank is a pill bug whose daily routine involves nibbling a dead leaf, climbing up a long stick, avoiding a skateboarder, and playing pretend with his best friend, a human girl named Amelia. Identifiers: LCCN 2015036910 | ISBN 978-0-553-51150-5 (hardback) | ISBN 978-0-553-51151-2 (glb) | ISBN 978-0-553-51152-9 (ebk) Subjects: | CYAC: Woodlice (Crustaceans)—Fiction. | Human-animal relationships—Fiction. | Best friends—Fiction. | Play—Fiction. | BISAC: JUVENILE FICTION / Animals / Insects, Spiders, etc. | JUVENILE FICTION / Nature & the Natural World / General (see also headings under Animals). | JUVENILE FICTION / Social Issues / Self-Esteem & Self-Reliance. Classification: LCC PZ7.K9490113 Han 2016 | DDC [E]—dc23

The text of this book is set in Regula.
The illustrations were rendered digitally.

MANUFACTURED IN CHINA

2 4 6 8 10 9 7 5 3 1

First Edition

Random House Children's Books supports the First Amendment and celebrates the right to read.

Story by *Evan Kuhlman*
Pictures by *Chuck Groenink*

schwartz & wade books • new york

A big rock.

Hank, a pill bug, crawls out from under.

Hank shimmies through tall grass.

He nibbles on a dead leaf.

Breakfast over,
Hank creeps past
a cricket.

He comes upon a worm tied in a knot . . .

and an ant carrying a potato chip.

A curious cricket
A weird worm

Yikes!

A scary
grasshopper

Hank climbs a long stick.

He continues climbing the stick.

He finishes climbing the stick.

Then he curls up in the tall grass.

Hank scoots along and finds himself on a sidewalk. He looks both ways, then starts to cross.

He lumbers through a pothole.

He stops to inspect a rainbow made of chalk.

Some stripey art

He climbs on top of a bottle cap.

Hank finishes crossing as a boy rides by on a skateboard.

Too close for comfort!

Hank trudges onward and comes upon a smiling face.

She is dressed up like her hero, the famous flier Amelia Earhart.

Hank's best friend, Amelia

With Amelia's help, Hank crawls onto her helmet.

Amelia jumps up, tilts her arms, and takes off, with Hank aboard.

Amelia and her copilot, Hank the pill bug, are crossing the Atlantic Ocean in their airplane.

Together, they run around the front yard.

An amazing view of the world!

The brave pilots fly over England and wave to the queen. "Hello, Queen!"

Amelia and Hank zip through the side yard. Amelia's dog is fast asleep in her doghouse.

The fliers circle a maple tree and head for a picnic table.

Hank nibbles a peppermint leaf and Amelia drinks from a juice box.

In Paris, the plane just misses the Eiffel Tower. Amelia lands near a café, Le Velvet Bug.

Yum!

Snack break over, Amelia puts out her hand and Hank crawls back on board.

They run across the yard and down the driveway. Amelia's brother Aaron is playing with his army guys.

Amelia sets Hank on the mossy rock where she found him.

Hank gazes up at Amelia.

What friendship looks like

Hank crosses the sidewalk,

curls up and
plays dead,

and passes the grasshopper,

treks down his
exercise stick,

the ant, the worm, and the cricket.

Then he takes a big bite out of a dead leaf.

And when day is done,
Hank crawls under his rock at last.

Home, sweet home